The big Surprise

Written and illustrated by

David Bennett

BARRON'S
New York

This is Ben and the Baby Gang.
Today is Ben's birthday.
Mom and Dad have hidden his present
somewhere in the garden.

The twins, Sam and Kate, can't wait
to help Ben look for the present.
Lucy and Woolly are off already!

"Let's look in the shed," said Ben.

"I'm going to get there first," shouted Sam.
"Woof," barked Woolly.

They looked inside the shed,
but they couldn't see a present anywhere.
Woolly was outside, wagging his tail.
"I think Woolly has found it," said Sam.

"No, he hasn't," said Kate,
"It's only an old bone."
"Let's go and look in the flowerbeds," said Sam.

Lucy had crawled over
to a big bush.
She had found a long, red ribbon.

"What does Lucy have?" asked Sam.

"Look in the bush, Ben," said Kate.

"I can see something," said Ben.

"It's my present," cried Ben.

"Clever Lucy!" shouted the Gang.

"Quick, let's open it!" said Sam.

They ripped off the paper.
"What a big box!" said Ben.
"I wonder what's inside?"

"I think it's a giant, furry, green monster
with pink eyes," said Kate.

"Maybe it's an elephant with two trunks,"
suggested Sam.

"I hope it's a big airplane," said Ben,
"one that goes around and around
and around."

Suddenly, Woolly came rushing past,
chasing the cat from next door.
"Be careful of my present!" shouted Ben.

Crash!

The box tumbled over.

The Gang could hear lots of loud noises.

WHIZZ, BANG, POP, BUZZ!

WHIZZ, BANG, POP, BUZZ!

boing!

Suddenly the box burst open.
Out whizzed something strange.
"Look!" said Lucy.

"It's a robot!" shouted Ben,
    jumping up and down with excitement.
"Quick, after it!" shouted Sam.

The Gang marched after the robot,
laughing and giggling.

WHIZZ, BANG, POP, BUZZ!
WHIZZ, BANG, POP, BUZZ!

The Gang rushed inside the house.
Ben carried his new robot.
Mom had made a lovely birthday party.

"Happy birthday to you, happy birthday to you,"
sang the Gang.
Ben smiled and poured a cup of lemonade
for his robot.

"This is the best surprise present in the whole world," said Ben.

First edition for the United States
published 1989 by Barron's Educational Series, Inc.,
250 Wireless Boulevard, Hauppauge, New York 11788.

Copyright © 1988 by Conran Octopus Limited.

First published in 1988 by
Conran Octopus Limited, London, England.

Library of Congress Catalog Card No. 88-17055

International Standard Book No. 0-8120-5912-3

Printed by Eagle Press, Scotland
890   987654321